Sleepyhead Bear

Story by **Lisa Westberg Peters**   Pictures by **Ian Schoenherr**

Greenwillow Books
An Imprint of HarperCollinsPublishers

Sleepyhead Bear
Text copyright © 2006 by Lisa Westberg Peters
Illustrations copyright © 2006 by Ian Schoenherr
All rights reserved. Manufactured in China.
www.harperchildrens.com

Ink and acrylic paint on watercolor paper
were used for the full-color art.
The text type is 42-point OPTI Hobble Oldstyle.

Library of Congress Cataloging-in-Publication Data
Peters, Lisa Westberg.
Sleepyhead bear / by Lisa Westberg Peters ;
pictures by Ian Schoenherr.
  p. cm.
"Greenwillow Books."
Summary: Bear tries to catch a few winks
in his lair, but all sorts of bugs are bugging him.
ISBN-10: 0-06-059675-9 (trade bdg.)
ISBN-13: 978-0-06-059675-0 (trade bdg.)
ISBN-10: 0-06-059676-7 (lib. bdg.)
ISBN-13: 978-0-06-059676-7 (lib. bdg.)
[1. Bears—Fiction. 2. Insects—Fiction. 3. Sleep—Fiction.
4. Stories in rhyme.] I. Schoenherr, Ian, ill. II. Title.
PZ8.3.P443Sl 2006 [E]—dc22 2005014877

First Edition 10 9 8 7 6 5 4 3 2 1

Greenwillow Books

For my nieces,
Melissa and Chandra
—L. W. P.

For Rivers and his uncle Sam
—I. S.

Under sizzling skies
with hot air to spare,
Bear tries to catch
a few winks in his lair.

A bug buzzes here,
a bug buzzes there.

Poor little
ready-for-bed,
sleepyhead
Bear!

He tries to look tall and growls,

GRRRRRR!

But the bugs aren't afraid,
and they *buzzzzzz* in his fur.

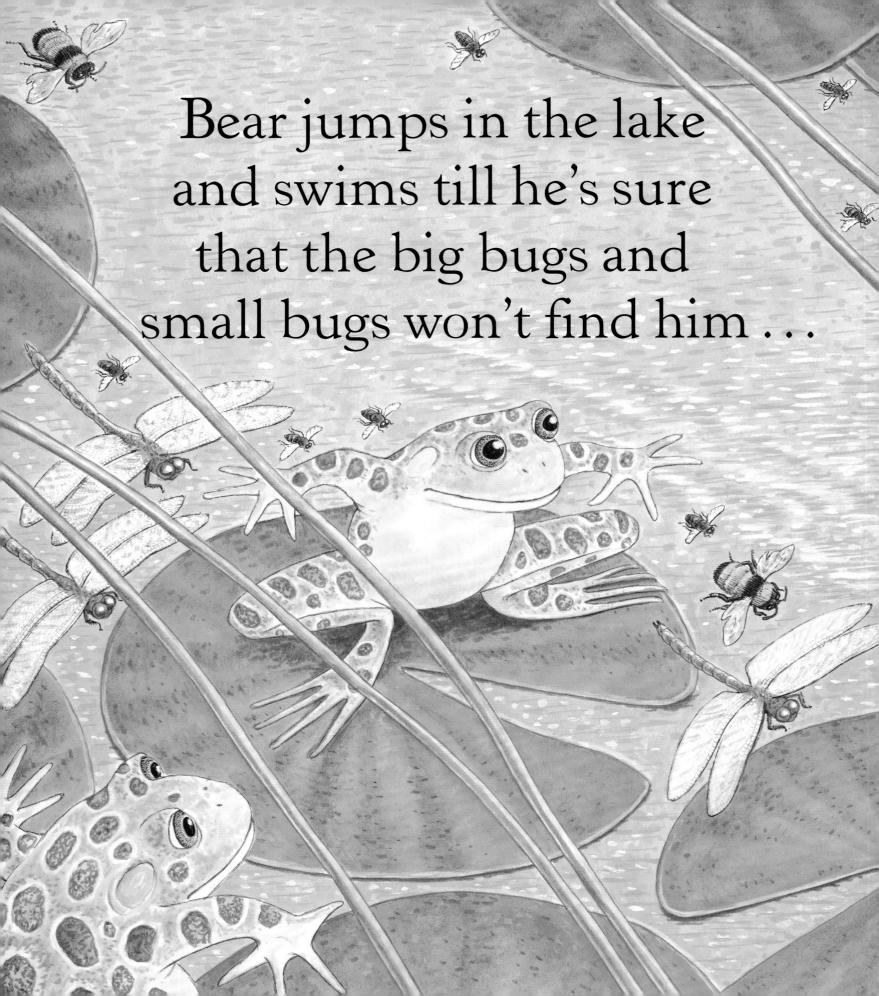

Bear jumps in the lake
and swims till he's sure
that the big bugs and
small bugs won't find him . . .

WHIRRRRRR!

Swat swat here,
slap slap there.

Poor little dog-paddling, frog-scattering Bear.

He climbs up a tree
but he doesn't get far,
because this is the tree
where the stinging bugs are!

He discovers a place to hide, but four raccoons won't budge until Bear says,

Raccoons flying here,
raccoons flying there.

Poor little
stuck-inside,
a-bit-too-wide
Bear!

The log starts to roll
down a hill, and it's clear
that Bear is going for a ride . . .

oh, dear!

The log turns around
and around before
Bear is tossed out,
dizzy and sore.

He lands in a meadow.
Poor little Bear
has bumps on his head,
bumps everywhere!

Too tired to climb up
and fall down anymore,
he lets out a squeaky
growl and roar.

Where are the bugs?
Did they disappear?
Maybe there aren't
any bugs down here.

Just flowers ... ah!

All of a sudden
Bear is a-blur
with bugs that don't buzz
or sting or whir.

Flutter and dip,
flutter and stir.
Bugs on his nose,
bugs on his fur.

They tickle away
his growl and his roar.
They tickle him till
he forgets he's sore.

Bear stands up straight
like a furry brown flower.
His new friends visit him
hour after hour.

Nodding off here,
nodding off there.

Dear little
fast-asleep,
at-last-asleep
Bear.

Under soft summer skies
with stars galore,
a warm breeze carries
the hint of a snore.